MW01028440

HOW COME CHRISTMAS

BOOKS BY

ROARK BRADFORD

OL' MAN ADAM AN' HIS CHILLUN

OL' KING DAVID AN', THE PHILISTINE BOYS

JOHN HENRY

KINGDOM COMING

HOW COME CHRISTMAS

LET THE BAND PLAY DIXIE

THIS SIDE OF JORDAN

THE THREE-HEADED ANGEL

HOW COME

A MODERN MORALITY

With Illustrations by PETER BURCHARD

CHRISTMAS

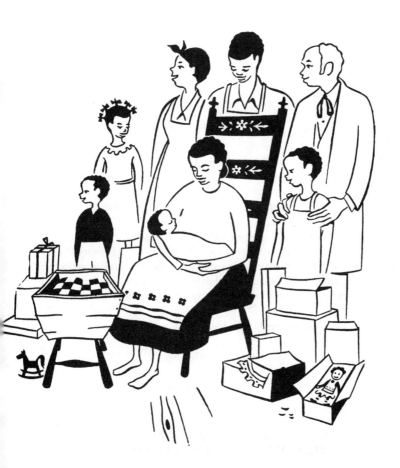

By ROARK BRADFORD

Cherokee Publishing Company
Atlanta, Georgia
1993

Library of Congress Cataloging-in-Publication Data

This book is printed on acid-free paper which conforms to the American National Standard Z39.48-1984 *Permanence of Paper for Printed Library Materials*. Paper that conforms to this standard's requirement for pH, alkaline reserve and freedom from groundwood is anticipated to last several hundred years without significant deterioration under normal library use and storage conditions.

Manufactured in the United States of America

ISBN: 0-87797-208-7

98 97 96 95 93   10 9 8 7 6 5 4 3 2 1

 Cherokee Publishing Company
PO Box 1730, Marietta, Georgia 30061

HOW COME CHRISTMAS

SCENE

You must imagine a corner in a rural negro church, by the stove. The stove is old, and the pipe is held approximately erect by guy-wires, but a cheerful fire is evident through cracks in the stove, and the wood-box is well filled. Six children sit on a bench which has been shifted to face the stove, and the Reverend stands between them and the stove. A hatrack supports sprigs of holly and one "plug" hat. A window is festooned with holly, long strips of red paper, and strings of popcorn. A small Christmas bell and a tiny American flag are the only "store bought" decorations.

HOW COME CHRISTMAS

REVEREND

WELL, hyar we is, chilluns, and hyar hit is Christmas. Now we all knows we's hyar 'cause hit's Christmas, don't we? But what I want to know is, who gonter tell me how come hit's Christmas?

1

'Cause old Sandy Claus come around about dis time er de year, clawin' all de good chilluns wid presents.

Dat ain't right, is hit, Revund? Hit's Christmas 'cause de Poor Little Jesus was bawned on Christmas, ain't hit, Revund?

Well, bofe er dem is mighty good answers. Old Sandy Claus do happen around about dis time er de year wid presents, and de Poor Little Jesus sho was bawned on Christmas Day. Now, de question is, did old Sandy Claus start clawin' chillun wid presents before de Poor Little Jesus got bawned, or did de Little Jesus git bawned before old Sandy Claus started gittin' around?

I bet old Sandy Claus was clawin' chilluns

before de Poor Little Jesus started studdin'
about gittin' bawned.

Naw, suh. De Little Jesus comed first, didn't
he, Revund?

Old Sandy Claus is de oldest. I seed his
pitchers and I seed Jesus' pitchers and old
Sandy Claus is a heap de oldest. His whiskers mighty nigh tetch de ground.

Dat ain't right. Old Methuselah is de oldest,
ain't he Revund? 'Cause de Bible say:

> Methuselah was de oldest man of his time.
> He lived nine hund'ed and sixty-nine.
> And he died and went to heaven in due time.

Methuselah was powerful old, all right.

He wa'n't no older den old Sandy Claus, I
bet. Old Sandy Claus got a heap er whiskers.

CHRISTINE

But de Poor Little Jesus come first. He was hyar before old man Methuselah, wa'n't he, Revund?

REVEREND

He been hyar a powerful long time, all right.

WILLIE

So has old Sandy Claus. He got powerful long whiskers.

DELIA

Moses got a heap er whiskers, too.

REVEREND

Yeah, Moses was a mighty old man, too, but de p'int is, how come Christmas git started bein' Christmas? Now who gonter tell me? 'Cause hyar hit is Christmas Day, wid ev'y-body happy and rejoicin' about, and hyar is us, settin' by de stove in de wa'm church-house, tawkin' about hit. But ain't nobody got no idee how come hit start bein' Christ-mas?

4

WILLIE

You can't fool old Sandy Claus about Christmas. He know, don't he Revund? He just lay around and watch and see how de chilluns mind dey maw, and den de fust thing you know he got his mind make up about who been good and who been bad, and den he just hauls off and has hisse'f a Christmas.

CHRISTINE

Yeah, but how come he know hit's time to haul off and have hisse'f a Christmas?

WILLIE

'Cause any time old Sandy Claus make up his mind to have Christmas, well, who gonter stop him?

CHRISTINE

Den how come he don't never make up his mind ontwell de middle er winter? How come he don't make up his mind on de Fou'th er July? Ev'ybody git good around de Fou'th er July, jest like Christmas, so's dey kin go to de

5

picnic. But Sandy Claus ain't payin' no mind to dat 'cause hit ain't time for Christmas, is hit, Revund?

WILLIE

Cou'se he don't have Christmas on de Fou'th er July. 'Cause hit ain't no p'int in Sandy Claus clawin' ev'body when ev'body's goin' to de picnic, anyhow. Sandy Claus b'lieve in scatterin' de good stuff out, don't he, Revund? He say, "Well, hit ain't no p'int in me clawin' fo'ks when dey already havin' a good time goin' to de picnic. Maybe I better wait to de dead er winter when hit's too cold for de picnic." Ain't dat right, Revund?

REVEREND

Sandy Claus do b'lieve in scatterin' de good stuff about de seasons, Willie, and hit sho ain't no p'int in havin' Christmas on de Fou'th er July. 'Cause de Fou'th er July is got hit's own p'int. And who gonter tell me what de p'int er de Fou'th er July is?

Old Gawge Wash'n'ton whupped de kaing,
And de eagle squalled, Let Freedom raing.

REVEREND

Dat's right. And dat was in de summertime,
so ev'ybody went out and had a picnic 'cause
dey was so glad dat Gawge Wash'n'ton
whupped dat kaing. Now what's de p'int er
Christmas?

WILLIE

Old Sandy Claus . . .

CHRISTINE

De Poor Little Jesus . . .

REVEREND

Well, hit seem like old Sandy Claus and
de Poor Little Jesus bofe is mixed up in dis
thing, f'm de way y'all chilluns looks at hit.
And I reckon y'all is just about zackly right,
too. 'Cause dat's how hit is. Bofe of 'em is
so mixed up in hit dat I can't tell which is
which, hardly.

8

DELIA

Was dat before de Fou'th er July?

CHRISTINE

Cou'se hit was. Don't Christmas always come before de Fou'th er July?

WILLIE

Naw, suh. Hit's de Fou'th er July fust, and den hit's Christmas. Ain't dat right, Revund?

REVERFND

I b'lieve Christine got you dat time, Willie. Christmas do come before de Fou'th er July. 'Cause you see hit was at Christmas when old Gawge Wash'n'ton got mad at de kaing 'cause de kaing was gonter kill de Poor Little Jesus. And him and de kaing fit f'm Christmas to de Fou'th er July before old Gawge Wash'n'ton finally done dat kaing up.

WILLIE

And Gawge Wash'n'ton whupped dat kaing, didn't he?

9

He whupped de stuffin' outn him. He whupped him f'm Balmoral to Belial and den back again. He jest done dat kaing up so bad dat he jest natchally put kaingin' outn style, and ev'y since den hit ain't been no more kaings to 'mount to much.

You see, kaings was bad fɔ'ks. Dey was mean. Dey'd druther kill you den leave you alone. You see a kaing wawkin' down de road, and you better light out across de field, 'cause de

kaing would wawk up and chop yo' haid off.
And de law couldn't tetch him, 'cause he was
de kaing.
So all de fo'ks got skeered er de kaing, 'cause
dey didn't know how to do nothin' about hit.
So ev'ybody went around, tryin' to stay on de
good side of him. And all er dat is how come
de Poor Little Jesus and old Sandy Claus got
mixed up wid gettin' Christmas goin'.
You see, one time hit was a little baby bawned
name' de Poor Little Jesus, but didn't nobody

know dat was his name yit. Dey knew he was a powerful smart and powerful purty little baby, but they didn't know his name was de Poor Little Jesus. So, 'cause he was so smart and so purty, ev'ybody thought he was gonter grow up and be de kaing. So quick as dat news got spread around, ev'ybody jest about bust to git on de good side er de baby, 'cause dey figure efn dey start soon enough he'd grow up likin' 'em and not chop they heads off.

So old Moses went over and give him a hund'ed dollars in gold. And old Methuselah went over and give him a diamond ring. And old Peter give him a fine white silk robe. And ev'ybody was runnin' in wid fine presents so de Poor Little Jesus wouldn't grow up and chop dey heads off.

Ev'ybody but old Sandy Claus. Old Sandy Claus was kind er old and didn' git around much, and he didn't hyar de news dat de Poor Little Jesus was gonter grow up and be de kaing. So him and de old lady was settin' back by de fire one night, toastin' they shins and tawkin' about dis and dat, when old Miz Sandy Claus up and remark, she say, "Sandy, I hyars Miss Mary got a brand-new baby over at her house."

"Is dat a fack?" say Sandy Claus. "Well, well, hit's a mighty cold night to do anything like dat, ain't hit? But on de yuther hand, he'll be a heap er pleasure and fun for her next summer, I reckon."

So de tawk went on, and finally old Sandy Claus remark dat hit was powerful lonesome around de house since all er de chilluns growed up and married off.

"Dey all married well," say Miz Sandy Claus, "and so I say, 'Good ruddance.' You ain't never had to git up and cyore dey colic and mend dey clothes, so you gittin' lonesome. Me, I love 'em all, but I'm glad dey's married and doin' well."

So de tawk run on like dat for a while, and

den old Sandy Claus got up and got his hat. "I b'lieve," he say, "I'll drap over and see how dat baby's gittin' along. I ain't seed no chillun in so long I'm pyore hongry to lean my eyes up agin a baby."

"You ain't goin' out on a night like dis, is you?" say Miz Sandy Claus.

"Sho I'm goin' out on a night like dis," say Sandy Claus. "I'm pyore cravin' to see some chilluns."

"But hit's snowin' and goin' on," say Miz Sandy Claus. "You know yo' phthisic been devilin' you, anyhow, and you'll git de chawley mawbuses sloppin' around in dis weather."

"No mind de tawk," say Sandy Claus. "Git me my umbrella and my overshoes. And you better git me a little somethin' to take along for a cradle gift, too, I reckon."

"You know hit ain't nothin' in de house for no cradle gift," say Miz Sandy Claus.

"Git somethin'," say Sandy Claus. "You got

to give a new baby somethin', or else you got bad luck. Get me one er dem big red apples outn de kitchen."

"What kind er cradle gift is an apple?" say Miz Sandy Claus. "Don't you reckon dat baby git all de apples he want?"

"Git me de apple," say Sandy Claus. "Hit ain't much, one way you looks at hit. But f'm de way dat baby gonter look at de apple, hit'll be a heap."

So Sandy Claus got de apple and he lit out.

Well, when he got to Miss Mary's house ev'ybody was standin' around givin' de Poor Little Jesus presents. Fine presents. Made outn gold and silver and diamonds and silk, and all like dat. Dey had de presents stacked around dat baby so high you couldn't hardly see over 'em. So when ev'ybody seed old Sandy Claus come in dey looked to see what he brang. And when dey seed he didn't brang nothin' but a red apple, dey all laughed. "Quick as dat boy grows up and gits to be de kaing," dey told him, "he gonter chop yo' haid off."

"No mind dat," say Sandy Claus. "Y'all jest stand back." And so he went up to de crib and he pushed away a handful er gold and silver and diamonds and stuff, and handed de Poor Little Jesus dat red apple. "Hyar, son," he say, "take dis old apple. See how she shines?"

And de Poor Little Jesus reached up and grabbed dat apple in bofe hands, and laughed jest as brash as you please!

Den Sandy Claus tuck and tickled him under de chin wid his before finger, and say, "Goodly-goodly-goodly." And de Poor Little Jesus laughed some more and he reached up and grabbed a fistful er old Sandy Claus's whiskers, and him and old Sandy Claus went round and round!

So about dat time, up stepped de Lawd. "I swear, old Sandy Claus," say de Lawd. "Betwixt dat apple and dem whiskers, de Poor

Little Jesus ain't had so much fun since he been bawn."

So Sandy Claus stepped back and bowed low and give de Lawd hy-dy, and say, "I didn't know ev'ybody was chiv-areein', or else I'd 'a' stayed at home. I didn't had nothin' much to bring dis time, 'cause you see how hit's been dis year. De dry weather and de bull weevils got mighty nigh all de cotton, and de old lady been kind er puny—"

"Dat's all right, Sandy," say de Lawd. "Gold and silver have I a heap of. But verily you sho do know how to handle yo'se'f around de chilluns."

"Well, Lawd," say Sandy Claus, "I don't know much about chilluns. Me and de old lady raised up fou'teen. But she done most er de work. Me, I jest likes 'em and I manages to git along wid 'em."

"You sho do git along wid 'em good," say de Lawd.

"Hit's easy to do what you likes to do," say Sandy Claus.

"Well," say de Lawd, "hit might be somethin' in dat, too. But de trouble wid my world is, hit ain't enough people which likes to do de right thing. But you likes to do wid chilluns, and dat's what I needs. So stand still and shet yo' eyes whilst I passes a miracle on you."

So Sandy Claus stood still and shet his eyes, and de Lawd r'ared back and passed a miracle on him and say, "Old Sandy Claus, live forever, and make my chilluns happy."

So Sandy Claus opened his eyes and say, "Thank you, kindly, Lawd. But do I got to keep 'em happy all de time? Dat's a purty big job. Hit'd be a heap er fun, but still and at de same time—"

"Yeah, I knows about chilluns, too," say de Lawd. "Chilluns got to fret and git in devilment ev'y now and den and git a whuppin' f'm dey maw, or else dey skin won't git loose so's dey kin grow. But you jest keep yo' eyes on 'em and make 'em all happy about once a year. How's dat?"

"Dat's fine," say Sandy Claus. "Hit'll be a heap er fun, too. What time er de year you speck I better make 'em happy, Lawd?"

"Christmas suit me," say de Lawd, "efn hit's all o.k. wid you."

"Hit's jest about right for me," say old Sandy Claus.

So ev'y since dat day and time old Sandy Claus been clawin' de chilluns on Christmas, and dat's on de same day dat de Poor Little Jesus got bawned. 'Cause dat's de way de Lawd runs things. O' cou'se de Lawd knowed hit wa'n't gonter be long before de Poor Little Jesus growed up and got to be a man. And when he done dat, all de grown fo'ks had him so's dey c'd moan they sins away and lay they burdens down on him, and git happy in they hearts. De Lawd made Jesus for de grown fo'ks. But de Lawd know de chilluns got to have some fun, too, so dat's how come hit's Sandy Claus and Christmas and all.